BURIED BONES AND
TROUBLESOME TREASURE

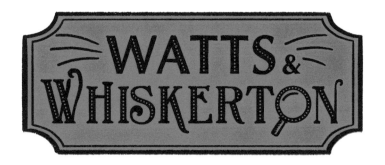

WATTS & WHISKERTON

BURIED BONES AND TROUBLESOME TREASURE

MEG McLAREN

Piccadilly
PRESS

First published in Great Britain in 2024 by
PICCADILLY PRESS
4th Floor, Victoria House, Bloomsbury Square, London WC1B 4DA
Owned by Bonnier Books
Sveavägen 56, Stockholm, Sweden
bonnierbooks.co.uk/PiccadillyPress

A CIP catalogue record for this book is available from the British Library.

ISBN: 978-1-80078-659-2
Also available as an ebook and in audio

1 3 5 7 9 10 8 6 4 2

Designed by Sarah Malley
Printed and bound in China

Piccadilly Press is an imprint of Bonnier Books UK
bonnierbooks.co.uk

extra
pencils
↓

book
↓

← bedtime
book

lunchbox
↓

For Jonny,

my perfect partner in crime

spare
notebook

notebook

my best
bow tie

torch

HERB
GARDEN

ROSES

POOL DIG SITE

HOUNDSTOOTH'S
COTTAGE

MAP OF
WHISKERTON MANOR

MUSEUM ⇨

Hello, my name is
Watts!

always curious

detecting hat

super hearing

notebook (I write everything down)

spare pencil (always have a backup)

plenty of pockets to put clues in

8¼ years old

I come from a family of detectives and I've travelled all over the world with my

my first case (aged 3 days)

MUMMY LOOSE ON BABY WARD

parents while they solve their curious cases. But Mum and Dad are so good at their job that I never got the chance to help. Which meant that I didn't know if I was a good detective too, or even if I wanted to be one, because I'd never tried anything else.

WATTS FAMILY RECOVER WORLD'S LARGEST DIAMOND

my fifth birthday ↗

So when my parents went searching for the Wishing Well of Wherever, I decided it was time for a change. I wanted to see what life was like when we weren't tracking down diamond thieves or locating long-lost loot. Also, I *really* didn't fancy going back to the jungle. I was looking forward to a week of doing whatever *I* wanted.

last time I was in the jungle

No, thanks!

But mysteries seem to follow my family around, and my holiday wasn't as relaxing as I'd hoped. Although I did finally get the chance to find out if I could solve a mystery on my own.

On your own? Wait, aren't I in this book?

This is my best friend,

Pearl

notices
everything

superrr
smart

asks A LOT
of questions

always right
(so she says!)

8½ years old
(likes to remind
me she's older)

no patience
whatsoever

always curious
to hear what I think

wants to be a detective

She's even keener on mysteries
than Mum and Dad!

And this is the story of how Pearl and I met. I wrote down everything that happened because I love to write. If I wasn't going to be a detective I wondered whether I could be a writer instead. As it turns out, my holiday gave me the perfect chance to practise both . . .

Ooh, a story about us! **Am I the hero?**

Let's read it and find out.

BURIED BONES
AND
TROUBLESOME TREASURE

NOTES

I had a **very early start** this morning.

The birds weren't even up yet!

Thankfully Dad packed me a sandwich.

I ate it two minutes after I got on the train

and I've been wishing I'd saved it ever since.

Luckily Mum also tucked a **sugary**

surprise into my suitcase.

So far the journey has been uneventful.

Cows and fields have replaced the busy

streets and tall buildings of home, so

we must be getting close now.

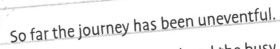

We've just pulled in to Little Gossip.

My **holiday** has officially begun!

CHAPTER ONE

THE BIG DIG

Whiskerton Manor was the biggest house I'd ever seen! While Mum and Dad were trudging through the rainforest, I was here to stay with Count Whiskerton, an old client of theirs who had volunteered to look after me. He had a daughter my age who was going to meet me at the gates.

9

Pearl took a very
deep breath and said . . .

sugar

jam

label

ticket

Please look after this Watts

11

'We'd better go,' said Pearl. 'We don't want to be late.'

I was glad we had been interrupted. Mum and Dad were the real detectives – I just tagged along. Pearl would be disappointed when she realised I wasn't quite as brilliant as them. But there was no time to worry about that now.

Late?
Late for **what?**

THE BIG DIG!

As we weaved our way through a huge crowd, Pearl explained that her dad was building a swimming pool and that a groundbreaking ceremony was about to begin. The manor gardens weren't usually open to the public so the whole village had jumped at the chance to have a look around.

Count Whiskerton stood proudly in front of a dazzling display of roses next to the lawn.

'Good afternoon, everyone!' he said, greeting
the crowd. 'As many of you know, I took up
swimming this year and I've taken to it like a
duck to, well, you know. But the village pond
has been a little crowded lately, so I've decided
to build my very own swimming pool.

'My daughter has informed me that it would be unneighbourly to keep the pool to myself and so the Whiskerton Paddling and Plunge Pool will be open to you all.

I'm so pleased that you could be here today as we take our first steps towards making my . . . I mean, *our* dream come true.'

I pulled my notebook out of my pocket. You never know when you might learn something useful or find an interesting detail to use in a story.

Is he going to dig the pool all by himself?

Oh, no. Dad's far too lazy for that. **Digby** will take over in a minute. Here she comes now.

rumble rumble

Digby was desperate to get started. She loved to dig. In fact, she lived for it.

DIGBY DIGGERS
WE LIVE TO DIG!

Hello, Digby. Ready to begin?

Oh, yes. I've been looking forward to this all week.

scribble scribble

How long will it take to dig the pool?

Count Whiskerton strode over to join us. 'Is this reporter bothering you, Digby? I thought I sent them all to tea. What newspaper did you say you're from?'

'He's not a reporter, Dad. He's a Watts. You invited him to stay. Remember?' said Pearl.

Ah, the detective boy! Your parents are marvels. I feel so much better now that there's a Watts around to keep an eye on things.

My stomach knotted. Everyone always assumes I'm a great detective because of my parents. But what if there really was trouble? What could *I* do about it?

'Now, you'll have to excuse me,' he said, 'I've got a swimming pool to dig. Ready, Digby?'

LET'S DIG!

As the engine roared into action, Count Whiskerton suddenly leaped in front of the digger, yelling for Digby to steer well clear of his precious prize-winning roses.

While we watched, Pearl asked, 'Do you write everything down?'

> *Erm, yes. When Mum and Dad are investigating they need to remember all sorts of **important details.** I write them all down in case they forget . . . but they never do.*

> *It's **not just the facts,** though. Writing helps me understand the world around me. I'm not sure I've inherited Mum and Dad's sleuthing skills. Maybe I'm just a **writer.***

Pearl sat quietly. Perhaps she'd only want to be my friend if I was a detective . . . But after a moment she smiled brightly.

> *I think you can be anything you want to be. Write this down, Watts: **digging is dull.** Come on, let me give you a tour of the house.*

MY ROOM! *It's going to be so great. We can stay up all night solving mysteries!*

Mysteries! No matter where I went I couldn't escape them.

Pearl's room was an explosion of hobbies. It was surprisingly like mine. I must've been quiet for too long because she suddenly said, 'Oh, but you don't want to solve mysteries. This must seem so dull to you. You've been on so many exciting adventures.'

'Exciting? The last time I was in the jungle I was nearly eaten alive,' I said. 'This is amazing! It's just been me and Mum and Dad investigating for so long, so it's nice to have someone my own age to talk to, and a chance to figure out what *I* like to do.'

As night fell,
I unpacked
my things
and Pearl kept
an eye on the
pool's progress.
'Digby will have
to stop soon.
My ears can't
take much more.
Are you sure
you're going to be all right
down there?' she said.

It's perfect.
It's like
camping.

'I've never been camping,' said Pearl. 'Dad doesn't like the outdoors. He's a house cat.'

'I've camped all over,' I said. 'Once we set up camp late at night by the River Twist. It was only when the sun came up that we realised we'd pitched our tent on a raft and were floating downstream!'

We both laughed.

'Indoor camping is much safer,' I said, and we set about making our own tent.

The rumbling stopped at last. We watched Digby pack up and leave for the night.

It had
been such
a fun day,
and now that
our tent was
complete we
settled down and
instantly fell . . .

zZZ

The next morning we were
awoken by a scream.

AAAARRGHHH!

We ran outside in our pyjamas to see what
all the fuss was about.

My roses!
*Who would do
such a thing?*

Pearl and I stared
at the roses and
then at each other.
We both shrugged.

'What's wrong, Dad? They look all right to us.'

'*All right?*' he replied. 'Yesterday they were PERFECT! Now look at this mess. Someone's been moving them.'

Don't worry, I'll get this straightened out right away.

Just then, Digby arrived, whistling happily to herself. She was most offended when Pearl asked if she'd touched the roses.

I most certainly did not! And I locked those gates tight behind me last night. Anyway, I don't see what all the fuss is about. They look fine to me. Now, if you don't mind, I've got some digging to do.

As Digby got to work, the rumbling started once again, but before the first scoop of dirt left the ground I noticed something glistening in the soil.

Pearl and I moved closer to investigate.

I don't think you'll be digging today, Digby. That looks like a **tooth!**

'Nonsense,' said Count Whiskerton. 'Back to work, everyone.'

'We can't move it!' cried Pearl. 'We'd be disturbing evidence. Isn't that right, Watts?'

I was horrified to see that everyone was staring at me. Pearl gave me a reassuring nod, so I tried to think what Mum and Dad would say if they were here.

Erm, that's right. We have to preserve the site until we know what we've found. We need to call an expert ... erm, a-a bone expert.

I'll phone a doctor right away.

*Don't be silly! We need someone who can identify **old** bones. We should ask the museum.*

Count Whiskerton called the museum to tell them about our find. Dr Pandora said she'd come over immediately.

'Imagine, Watts. A real-life archaeologist is coming to inspect our grounds!' squealed Pearl.

What's an **archaeologist?**

Fancy name for a digger is all.

An archaeologist learns about history by examining the objects they find in the ground.

Like I said, **fancy digging.**

Count Whiskerton returned, closely followed by a reporter who'd come to get an update on the pool. 'It seems you may have found a better story,' he said, eyeing the tooth.

As we waited for the museum expert to arrive, Pearl asked, 'Have you noticed any clues that might tell us what it is?'

I shook my head. 'Detective work is all about two things. Firstly, facts. I could guess what we've found, but we won't know for a *fact* until an expert examines it.'

'What's the second thing?' asked Pearl.

Patience.

Smudge Inkly, reporter

But that's my **least favourite** thing!

33

As promised, Dr Pandora (the fancy digger) soon arrived and brought her assistant, Dr Arty Fact, with her. He was a palaeontologist. That's someone who specialises in dinosaur bones.

After much discussion they confirmed that Pearl was right: Digby would have to wait.

Utterly fascinating!

WATTS' NOTES

Things have taken a very exciting turn here at Whiskerton Manor. We've discovered a **dinosaur tooth!** And Pearl and I might have a mystery to solve. I'm not sure how I feel about that yet since I came here to try something new.

THE FACTS

unhappy Digby

★ According to Count Whiskerton, his roses were **moved** in the night. (But Pearl and I think they look the same.)

QUESTIONS

★ Why would anyone move roses around?

Bye

we're moving!

CHAPTER TWO

GROUND-BREAKING NEWS! PREHISTORIC PRESENCE PROLONGS POOL PLANS!

Good morning, I'm Smudge Inkly...

After our unexpectedly early start, Pearl and I finally got dressed and sat down to breakfast. News of our discovery had spread far and wide.

I've heard enough! All my plans have been undone by a piece of rock.

It's not a rock, it's a historical find.

CRUNCH CRUNCH

'Well, I wish they hadn't historically found it here. It's getting in the way of my swimming pool!' said Count Whiskerton as he stormed out of the room.

There was a nice photo of Count Whiskerton in the paper. It was a shame his front-page pool story was already old news. I asked Pearl if she thought someone really had moved his roses.

'They didn't move them far if they did. And now Dad will make sure no one gets in! Come on, let's take that toast to go,' said Pearl, ushering me out of the door.

Keep your eyes peeled, Houndstooth. You **patrol** the grounds and I'll double-check the gates are locked.

Outside, Dr Pandora had been busy.

I was surprised by how much the archaeological team had already uncovered. Dr Arty Fact offered to show us around.

This could be a **major discovery.** The bones we're uncovering are **very** old. We have to be careful and work methodically.

A grid is laid out so we know exactly where we find each piece.

We move across the grid in order to make sure we don't miss anything.

PEG STRING

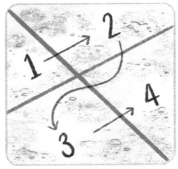

1 2 3 4

Brush Brush Brush

CLICK!

Dr Pandora brushes the soil away very gently.

I photograph and label everything we find.

'Then we'll take it all back to the museum where we'll reassemble the dinosaur.'

'What type is it?' asked Pearl. 'Could there be more than one?'

'It's too early to tell,' said Arty. 'We're just lucky that they started digging here, otherwise it may have gone undiscovered.'

'It's a little bit like solving a mystery, isn't it?' I said. 'You need all the facts before you can find a solution.' Pearl looked at me proudly.

We're **detectives**, you know. Well, I am. Watts hasn't decided yet.

Detectives? That's interesting...

Arty waved goodbye and went back to help Dr Pandora. He promised we could come to the museum to watch the bones being reassembled.

'How exciting is that?' said Pearl. 'We'll have front-row seats to a dinosaur skeleton.'

But all I could think about was what Arty had said. It *was* very lucky that the pool was being dug exactly where the dinosaur was found, right next to the roses . . .

Watts, you're not listening.

Sorry, I was thinking about the **roses** again. Let's take a closer look.

Pearl said, 'For someone who doesn't know if he's a detective you sure are curious.'

We inspected the rose bed carefully but didn't find anything out of the ordinary. If only there was a way to prove they'd been moved . . .

'Dad's got more pictures of these roses than he has of me,' Pearl said, laughing.

'Pearl, you're a genius!'

switched

I held the newspaper photo of Count Whiskerton by the roses. He was right and now we had proof. Some of them *had* switched places!

Yes! A real-live mystery to solve. Write this down: **Pearl and Watts are on the case!** Hmm... We need to think of a catchier name.

Now that there was officially a mystery to solve, this was my chance to find out if I really was a detective, or just the son of detectives. But I was glad I wouldn't have to do it alone.

We inspected the plants that had been moved more closely.

Oi! *What's all this then?*

As we explained what we were doing to Houndstooth, Digby made a discovery.

*Look at these marks in the soil. A spade would make a **clean** slice but whoever dug up these flowers didn't use one.*

They were claw marks!

'I don't know why they didn't use a spade,' said Digby. 'Even a natural digger like me knows that tools make a job easier. If you're allowed to get on with your job, that is.' She sighed deeply and went back to sit on her digger.

I wondered if the roses had been moved to help them grow better, but Houndstooth said they hadn't moved far enough for the soil conditions to have changed. He picked up his watering can and said, 'It's a mystery.'

He was right about that.

Pearl was smiling at me. 'What?' I asked.

'We've just made another discovery, thanks to you. You can't deny you're a natural detective.'

'Beginner's luck,' I replied, shrugging off the compliment.

But secretly I wondered if what Pearl said could be true. I'd learned a lot from my parents over the years, but it wasn't only that. I couldn't help but think over every little detail. My mind wandered back to the case.

The only explanation is that the intruder must have been looking for something in the rose bed. The question is, did they find it?

Let's keep an eye on it tonight in case they come back.

LATER THAT EVENING...

Keep your eyes peeled, Watts. Our rose-bush bandit could show up at any moment.

Let's discuss the case to keep us awake.

I am awake...

Pearl nudged me and then continued. 'The facts: someone is moving Dad's roses. Where? The garden. When? At night. Why? We don't know. How do we work out who it is?'

'Mum and Dad narrow down their suspects.'

Good idea. How do we do that?

Watts?

Watts!

We have to think about who had access. The whole village was here yesterday.

Yes, but the roses were moved at night when the gates were locked.

So only someone inside... **ZZZ...**

WATTS!

Snort... *It has to be someone inside the gates or someone who has a key or...*

Before I knew it I'd fallen asleep.

51

Luckily Pearl was awake enough for the both of us and had spotted some suspicious activity outside.

We hurried downstairs and peeked out of the front door.

The moment we stepped onto the grass a voice cried, 'Aha! I've caught you, you scoundrel!' and we found ourselves trapped.

It turns out we weren't the only ones who'd been keeping watch. Count Whiskerton had seen the torchlight too.

Suddenly we heard a bark and a rustle in the bushes. Someone was still out there! Together we moved closer and ducked behind the roses. On the count of three we pounced. The last person we expected to find was . . .

'I was checking on the roses when I noticed someone starting to dig,' he said. 'When I barked they ran away.'

Pearl shone her light where two rose bushes should have been.

Pearl nudged me.

'Look at Houndstooth's pocket,' she whispered. 'Is it just me or does that look like . . .'

'A bone!'

Had Houndstooth disturbed an intruder before they'd found what they were looking for, or had *we* disturbed Houndstooth?

COME ON, YOU TWO, IT'S VERY LATE.

We took one last look at the freshly disturbed soil. It was just like before: claw marks.

NOTES

It's been a fascinating day. Pearl and I learned

lots about archaeology, and we now have

proof that Count Whiskerton's roses were

history
_by_
digging moved. Pearl is thrilled to have a mystery to

solve, and although I came here to have a

break from detective work, I'm starting to

PROOF

enjoy investigating.

THE FACTS

★ Some flowers have **switched places**

while some whole bushes have been dug up.

switched   dug up

★ The soil was dug with **claws**.

QUESTIONS

★ Why were the rose bushes moved?

★ Who is our clawed digger?

★ Why did Houndstooth have a **bone**

in his pocket?

The next morning I decided to make an early start.

But before I had a chance to explain, Arty arrived and asked if we'd like to go to the museum to see the first batch of bones being assembled.

'Notebook at the ready, Watts,' whispered Pearl as we climbed into the car. 'You never know when a clue will turn up.'

At the bottom of the drive Arty pulled a key from his pocket and unlocked the gates. As we drove off, Pearl told him about last night's events.

Have you seen the dinosaur?

← REPORTERS →

'Not again?' said Arty. 'Your father must be so upset.'

WHY?

sob

'You could say that,' she replied.

Pearl was so excited about visiting the museum that she soon forgot about the case.

How old is the museum?

Is it older than the bones?

Have you ever unearthed **an ancient museum?**

Is there a **museum of ancient museums?**

How do they fit them all inside?

Brm Brm

I tried to refocus the conversation.

Were any bones missing this morning?

Arty shook his head. Everything at the dig was just as they had left it.

Arty sounded relieved when he said,

HERE WE ARE!

Museum

and he got out of the car before Pearl could ask any more questions. We hadn't learned much about the case, but one point did stick out. I scribbled a note and showed it to Pearl.

IF NO BONES ARE MISSING FROM THE DIG, WHERE DID HOUNDSTOOTH GET ONE?

The museum was even more wondrous than I'd imagined. It was a cavernous space full of treasures.

63

While Arty unpacked the bones, Pearl and I explored the exhibits.

'Ooh, that reminds me,' said Pearl, taking my notebook. She flicked through the pages and showed me what she'd been working on last night after I'd fallen asleep.

'Is that a list of suspects?'

'Yes, I've ruled out you, me and Dad. That leaves Houndstooth inside the grounds. And Digby, who has a key.'

'Arty has one too,' I said, adding him to the list. 'I wonder if he shares it with Dr Pandora. I'd better add her too just in case.'

We stared at the four names. Who was guilty?

It was hard to focus in a building as fascinating as the museum, and our attention soon wandered.

Arty, who had returned to fetch us, told us all about the missing exhibit.

It was our greatest find. An apple made of **pure gold**, dating back 300 years, discovered buried beneath desert sands.

GONE!

The night before it went on display it was **stolen**. The police search was fruitless. Even the staff were under suspicion!

NOT HERE.

NOT IN HERE.

The apple was never found.

WE'RE INNOCENT!

'I bet *we* could find it,' said Pearl.

But we already had enough mysteries to solve, including what kind of dinosaur we had found . . .

The back rooms of the museum weren't as impressive as the front, or as organised. There was dust everywhere.

'If we get lost, we can follow Arty's footprints,' whispered Pearl.

You mean claw marks.

Excuse the mess. We've had a break-in.

'A break-in!' I exclaimed.

'Was anything stolen?' asked Pearl.

'That's the curious thing,' said Arty. 'Both door locks were broken but nothing appears to be missing.'

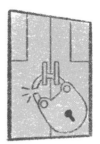

FRONT DOOR

I looked at the dusty jumble of artefacts around me and wondered how anyone would know if anything had been stolen.

STORE ROOM

Hmmm

Come on, Watts. We've got a dinosaur to build!

Building a dinosaur is like solving an enormous jigsaw. Arty moved each bone carefully, trying them in different positions to see where they fitted. I noticed he was struggling to find which pieces went together.

Do you know what kind of dinosaur it is yet?

'No, some of the bones fit together while others seem out of place,' said Arty. 'It must be a creature I haven't seen before . . .'

A new species? That's exciting.

I suppose it is.

But Arty didn't sound excited.

Arty asked if we'd like to take a closer look at one of the bones. Of course

distinctive break

fibula (leg bone)

we said yes, but as he passed it to us, I had the strangest feeling. I thought back carefully. I'd seen Arty holding the same bone only minutes ago.

On our way out of the museum I showed the photograph to Pearl. She pressed her nose against the glass and muttered . . .

It can't be the same bone. Dr Pandora only dug it up this morning. I'm sure they all just look alike . . .

My heart sank. This is why I didn't want to get involved in detective work. I knew I'd be no good at it.

I braced myself, waiting for Pearl to tell me that I was wrong. Instead she surprised me.

If this is the same bone, what does that mean?

It means that at least one of the bones in your garden has been found by Arty before!

There was so much to see at the museum! We learned all about the Apple of Cordovia AND a recent break-in. I hope they don't come back for our bones. But the strangest thing is that one of the bones in the museum photographs looks exactly like one that was dug up in Pearl's garden.

THE FACTS

★ The museum was <u>broken into</u> recently.

★ An expensive exhibit was stolen last year.

QUESTIONS

★ Why would someone break into the museum and not take anything?

★ Who took the Apple of Cordovia?

★ Could the garden bone be the one in the photo?

★ Where did Houndstooth get the bone in his pocket from?

CRAYON

CHAPTER FOUR

*Roses are red,
Violets are blue,
What have we found?
It must be a **clue!***

Pearl and I took the bus home.

'Something very fishy is going on here, Watts. Instead of one mystery we have four:

1. Dad's roses

2. The museum break-in

3. The double-dug-up dinosaur bone

4. The Lost Apple of Cordovia

Where do we begin?' she asked.

Erm ... I'm not sure. What do you think?

Come on, Watts. I want to know what **you** think.

That's how this works. It takes two of us. I **think up** ideas and you try them.

I have **SO** many questions!

I only have one.

I ask a million questions, but you ask **exactly** the right one.

I want to solve four mysteries at once but you think carefully about what to do next. We're so different. That's what makes us such a **purr-fect** team!

I was used to accompanying Mum and Dad on cases, but I'd never felt like part of a team before. It was nice. And Pearl was right – I *did* know what to do next.

Pearl looked disappointed when I told her we couldn't solve four cases at once. It was best to focus on the one closest to home: the roses.

'All our suspects have access to the garden, but we need to check if they all have keys to the gate,' Pearl said.

'We've also discovered that the digger is leaving claw marks behind,' I said. 'All our suspects have claws.'

'But I've never seen Digby without gloves.'

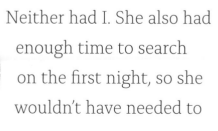

Neither had I. She also had enough time to search on the first night, so she wouldn't have needed to return. I scored Digby off the suspect list and turned my attention to Houndstooth. Where had he got that bone from?

'Let's ask him when we get back,' said Pearl.

I was about to put my notebook away when I saw the drawing I'd made earlier. As I held it up for Pearl to see –

DING! DING!

Watts, this is our stop.

I tucked my notebook away and forgot all about it.

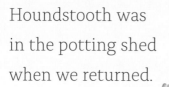

Houndstooth was in the potting shed when we returned.

We asked him what equipment we'd need if we wanted to start gardening. Secretly we were trying to find out more about the case.

Well, you'd definitely need

a trowel

soil

seeds

pots

gloves

a watering can...

'Can't we just dig with our paws?' I asked.

'Oh, no,' he replied. 'Plants are very delicate – you've got to take care if you want them to grow.'

'Look,' said Pearl impatiently, 'we need to ask about the bone you had last night.'

'B-b-bone?'

I pointed at his pocket. 'We know it's not from the dig.'

'Don't worry,' I told him. 'I still play with toys too.' We left him to his plants.

As we wandered through the herb garden
I thought about why the roses were being
dug up at night.

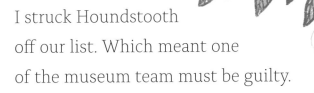

I struck Houndstooth off our list. Which meant one of the museum team must be guilty.

'But their work is so delicate, I can't imagine them clawing at the ground,' I said. 'And they didn't have keys to the gate on the first night. They arrived the next morning.'

SAGE

Hmmm, true, but maybe Digby forgot to lock the gates after the ceremony – it *was* a busy day!

MINT

We need to talk to Dr Pandora next and see what we can find out from her.

Suspects
~~Houndstooth~~
~~Digby~~
Dr Arty Fact
Dr Pandora

83

With Arty still at the museum, it was the perfect chance to speak to Dr Pandora alone.

Let's ask about the roses and see how she reacts. And look to see if she's wearing gloves. **We'll ask about the museum break-in too and the Apple of Cordovia and –**

*Pearl, you're trying to solve **all four cases** again!*

Okay . . . gloves and roses.

Pearl immediately abandoned our plan.

While Pearl was down in the trench asking questions, I stayed on ground level where I had a perfect view. Here's what I discovered . . .

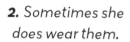

1. *Sometimes Dr Pandora doesn't wear gloves.*

2. *Sometimes she does wear them.*

3. *She has her own key.*

4. *She's as organised as Arty.*

'You noticed all that just by standing here?' Pearl said as she joined me. 'I need to stand still more often!'

'But none of that helps us,' I said. 'They both have claws, keys and access to the museum and garden.'

We were no closer to discovering which of them was digging up the roses or why.

If the museum staff are keeping secrets, they're buried deeper than those bones.

I'd been over the evidence so many times I couldn't think straight. Pearl was looking through my notes for anything we'd missed. Suddenly she said, 'Is this a story?'

I tried to take my notebook from her, but she held it out of reach. 'Erm, it's not finished yet. I was writing about us solving the mystery.'

'It's about us? Now you have to let me read it! Please?'

'All right, but only the first few pages.'

It felt like forever before Pearl finally closed the book. 'You're a really great writer, Watts. But you're a good detective too.'

pace
pace

'They're sort of the same,' I said. 'Solving a mystery is just like writing a story.'

'How?' asked Pearl.

It doesn't matter if it's a story or a mystery – you simply look at all the people, what they've done and why they've done it, and that's how you know how it ends.

I think you're a great writer **because** you're a great detective. We're going to solve this case, and I can't wait to read how we do it!

Solving cases had never been this much fun before.

Come on, it must be dinnertime.

Count Whiskerton had hardly touched his food. Instead he was looking through an old photograph album.

My beautiful baby...

Are those photos of Pearl when she was a kitten?

He's talking about his other babies.

'They were so beautiful they put them in the *Gazette*,' said Count Whiskerton proudly.

I took the album from him and said, 'Pearl, you might want to take a look at this.'

Little. **Gossip Gazette** 50p

MUSEUM'S MISSING APPLE STILL MISSING

WHISKERTON WOWS WITH WOSES (ROSES)

PHOTOGRAPHED BEFORE THEFT

The roses were planted around the same time as the Apple of Cordovia was stolen. Could it be a coincidence?

Detectives don't believe in coincidences.

91

Count Whiskerton sighed.

Don't worry, Dad. Watts and I have got this all figured out ... nearly. Show Dad your drawing. That'll cheer him up.

I pulled out my notebook and tried to explain. 'It's not exactly a drawing. It's ...'

'Don't be modest, Watts. Look, Dad. Isn't it pretty?'

Count Whiskerton nodded. 'My poor roses. What will they do to them next?'

In that moment I realised I was holding a clue that could solve the whole case. I suggested we take our dinner outside.

'Nice day for a picnic, eh, Watts?' said Pearl.

'Never mind that. Look what I've discovered.'
I showed Pearl the drawing again.

'This confirms that it's one of the museum team,' said Pearl. 'But how does that help us?'

I smiled. 'Because now we know exactly where they'll dig next.'

WATTS, YOU'RE A GENIUS!

'You've cracked this case wide open! Why didn't you tell me earlier?'

'I didn't know it was a grid until your dad said, "What will they do to them next?" That's when I realised we can catch the digger in the act!'

It was time to set a trap.

WATTS' NOTES

We've **cracked the case!** Well, almost.

Pearl and I have set a trap. We need to wait

until it gets dark, then we'll know whodunnit.

THE FACTS

★ The rose-bush bandit is digging in a grid system.

It must be **Dr Arty Fact** or **Dr Pandora**.

★ We've seen both wearing gloves BUT Arty's

claws are on his feet and Dr Pandora takes her

gloves on and off. →

★ Both have a key to the garden and both have been

digging up bones that have been dug up before.

QUESTIONS

★ Who is **guilty**?

MUSEUM

★ What are they looking for?

★ Is it connected to the museum robberies?

★ How did they get in before they had a key?

CHAPTER FIVE

MARKS
THE SPOT

WE ARE HIDING HERE

We spent a busy evening putting our plan into action. Then we waited until night fell. We knew the intruder would come; we just had to be patient.

Where are they, Watts? We've been waiting forever!

They probably want to make sure we're all in bed.

Well, I wish they'd hurry up.

It wasn't long until we heard footsteps, the rustle of rose bushes and the scratching of earth.

CRUNCH! CRUNCH!
RUSTLE! RUSTLE!
SCRATCH! SCRATCH!

Pearl was fidgeting. 'Now?' she whispered.

I signalled for her to wait. We had to catch them red-handed. At last the digging stopped. I took a deep breath and yelled . . .

NOW!

Our torches flashed on and the blinding light revealed the identity of our culprit.

In her paws Dr Pandora held a glittering apple.

I finally found it. And I've lost it all over again.

We'd called the police ahead of time so they'd be there when we unveiled the culprit. They took the treasure from her.

It was only when she noticed that her paws were covered in glitter that Dr Pandora realised she'd dug up a fake. It's amazing what you can do with a piece of fruit and a jar of glitter!

Dr Pandora was taken back to the house for questioning.

103

'It all began with Count Whiskerton's roses,'
I said. 'Why would anyone dig them up?
It had to be someone with claws
and access to the garden. Once
we'd ruled out Digby
and Houndstooth,
we were left
with Dr Pandora
and Dr Arty Fact.'

'The break in the case came when Watts discovered the roses were being dug in a grid system,' Pearl continued. 'We knew how to catch our culprit because we knew where they'd dig next. That's when we decided to look more closely at the other mysteries we'd found out about. They were all connected.'

I explained that the museum had been broken into but nothing had been stolen.

FORCED OPEN

'Although how would you notice in all that mess?' asked Pearl.

CLUTTER

'Pearl, watch your manners!' said Count Whiskerton.

But that's what the thief was relying on. That no one would notice. We suspected that one of the bones from the garden had been dug up before.

GARDEN BONES

Today we compared the rest of the bones with the displays. All of them had been taken from the museum!

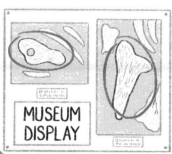

MUSEUM DISPLAY

107

'With the break-in solved we turned our attention to the Apple of Cordovia, a mystery I never imagined we'd crack. It had gone missing at the same time the roses were planted. What if that's what the mystery digger had been looking for all along?

NEXT ROSE BUSH IN THE GRID

Well, now that we knew where they would dig next, we could test our theory. There was only one thing standing in our way.'

You want to dig up my roses **AGAIN?!**

We promised it was the very last time.

Pearl explained our next step. 'We replaced the real apple with our glittery decoy and put our plan into action. We telephoned both our suspects and said, "Can you come in a bit later tomorrow? Dad wants some time to dig up his roses and move them to a safer part of the garden."'

'Whoever buried the apple would have to collect it tonight.'

By now the police had finished questioning Dr Pandora and had brought her into the room.

I can't believe it was you who took it. All this time.

The Apple of Cordovia was our **greatest discovery**. It should've been the pride of our collection, but it was worth a fortune.

I overheard the museum director agree to **sell it** to a private collector. I was furious because we'd worked so hard to find it. I couldn't let them take the apple away from us...

... so I made sure they wouldn't.

SMASH!

What I don't understand is why you buried it under my rose bushes?

The police immediately sniffed it was an inside job. It was only a matter of time before they discovered that I had the apple.

Where could I hide it? As I walked home that night I found the answer. There was a freshly dug hole in your garden.

HOUNDSTOOTH

WHISKERTON MANOR

I'll plant the roses first thing tomorrow.

Dr Pandora continued her story. 'The police soon lost the scent, but when I returned to Whiskerton Manor something had changed. I couldn't get the apple even if I wanted to.'

Don't these new gates look wonderful? My roses will be as safe as houses!

'And then last week I saw an article in the newspaper. It was my chance to get back into the grounds.'

An Announcement Is Announced!
Whiskerton Manor Welcomes You . . .
OPEN DAY!

FULL STORY PAGE 14

Diggin' for a livin'!

I attended the ceremony, but I stayed behind, hidden.

Who needs a spade?

DIG DIG DIG DIG DIG DIG

But I couldn't remember exactly where I'd buried the apple.

To give me more time to search I hid some bones from the museum to be found the next day.

random bones

I snuck out just before Digby locked the gate. I knew they'd call me to dig up the dinosaur.

We'll be over straight away!

Now I could come and go as I pleased. But my night-time digging was disturbed.

Who's there?

113

'You know the rest,' Dr Pandora finished.

'Poor Dr Pandora,' said Pearl as the archaeologist was taken away. 'She finally found her prize and we'd replaced it with a shiny fake.'

'I guess all that glitters isn't gold,' I said.

Arty was still stunned by Dr Pandora's confession. He shook his head sadly and went outside to gather the museum's bones before the police took them all.

grr

grr

grr

Bad, **bad boy!**

'It's a little disappointing not to have discovered a new dinosaur,' said Pearl, yawning widely. 'I guess we'll have to settle for finding a missing piece of priceless treasure.'

As we climbed the stairs to bed, Pearl asked, 'So what do you think, Watts? Are you a detective or a writer?'

'I'm a writer,' I said. Pearl's face fell.

'But,' I continued, '*we* are detectives. I wouldn't want to do it on my own.'

That's good news because we're an astounding duo. We were only wrong about one thing. Well, **you** were.

Me? Wrong?

You said we couldn't solve four mysteries at once,* but we have.

HAHA! HAHA! HAHA! HAHA! HAHA! HAHA!

* see page 78

The next day we were awoken early by the sound of rumbling.

ble rumble rumble rum

I have not missed this noise!

We traipsed drearily outside.

Let the Whiskerton Paddling and Plunge Pool dig begin... again!

Brm Brm

DIGBY DIGGERS
WE LIVE TO DIG

Scrape Scrape

As Digby took her first scoop I noticed something sticking out of the dirt.

It was a bone! Count Whiskerton nearly fainted. Digby stared in disbelief. 'Not another one!' they groaned.

I picked it up very carefully. Pearl gave it a gentle prod and it let out a wheeze of air.

It was no mystery who this bone belonged to. And, with that, the case was closed.

So that's the story of how Pearl and I became best friends. It was a holiday I'll never forget because it turns out that solving mysteries is what I like to do. I'm a detective after all. And although I'm starting to believe that I could do it by myself, I know that I wouldn't want to. Pearl and I bring out the best in each other.

Well, what did you think?

*We are clever, aren't we? And we do make an **excellent** team.*

It's a pity we don't have a catchier name. 'Pearl and Watts' doesn't sound right. How about 'Pearl and Pup'?

I was thinking . . . **'Watts and Whiskerton'**.

That's **purr-fect**. I wonder what our next case will be.

The only thing I know for sure is we won't have to wait long to find it. Mysteries seem to follow me around.

Look out for
Watts and Whiskerton's
next mystery...
coming soon!